This book is for Isaac Cintra.
Happy reading, I hope that you enjoy it!

CHAPTER 1

Erika frowned as she looked at the handwritten poster on the wall of the girls' toilets.

Do **YOU** have
a **UNIQUE** talent?
Could you **WOW** the judges and
WIN the **BIG** prize?
If so, then bring yourself **AND**
your **TALENT** to the school
hall for the **BIG SHOW** on
Wednesday afternoon!

This was tricky. On the one hand, Erika had some quite literally **UNBELIEVABLE** talents. She could talk to animals and swim through rocks, she could ride on clouds and make objects appear and disappear. The problem was, she could only do these things in her dreams, which wasn't much good for the school talent show.

When it came to real life, Erika's unique talents amounted to:

1. Watching a dead fly for quite a long time

Last year Erika had wanted to get into the *World Records* book and decided that all you needed to do was pick something strange enough and you'd be in with a chance.

Unfortunately, there was an old lady in Mexico who had already stared at a dead fly for three days. ***Three days!*** How would you even stay awake for three days . . . ?

2. Basketball tricks

Erika definitely had skills in this area. Once, during a crucial game against their rival school, she had scored the deciding point in the last seconds of the match. Unfortunately she had been facing the wrong way and scored the winning point for the other team.

Erika sighed. The talent show was only two days away, so there wasn't even time to learn anything new. It would be fun watching the other acts though.

She was still staring thoughtfully at the poster when, suddenly, she felt a curious tingling on her chest. Erika looked furtively around to check that no one else was there, but the room was empty. She walked over to the mirror, opened her collar and pulled out the large, pulsing crystal that hung on a chain around her neck. In the mirror it shone and gleamed with a dazzling light; but in the actual room Erika's hand was empty.

This was why Erika had checked that she was alone. The magic crystal was her way of communicating with the **DREAM DEFENDERS** – the TOP-SECRET organization that looks out for people while they're asleep and dreaming.

Erika tapped the crystal three times and a beam of light shone out. Projected in the beam was a boy who stood about her height, but was made out of curling shadows, which faded away to nothing just below his knees.

'Silas!' exclaimed Erika.

'Wait – you do know I'm at school?'

'Yes,' replied the shadow boy. 'And I'm sorry, I don't want to disrupt your education. Learning is a vital part of the human experience and I—'

'I'm not actually in a lesson, Silas,' interrupted Erika. 'If I was then you'd be being beamed out in front of thirty other kids! And the TOP-SECRET **DREAM DEFENDERS** wouldn't be very top secret any more. It wouldn't even be BOTTOM SECRET. It basically wouldn't be a secret at all!'

'Ah, no, I suppose not . . .' replied Silas. '*Anyway*, I just wanted to give you a heads up. We're going to need your help on a mission tonight, so make sure you get to bed early – we're going to need a full Dreamcycle to crack this one!'

Erika's heart leaped. 'OK, will do. See you later!'

Silas smiled as he saluted Erika, and then he disappeared.

A thrill of excitement coursed through Erika as she put the crystal back under her shirt. *A new mission!* It felt like ages since she'd received a call from the **DREAM DEFENDERS**. She whistled happily as she washed her hands, then turned and walked out of the bathroom.

A door to one of the cubicles opened and a girl walked out, shaking her head slowly. 'Erika Delgano is *SO* strange . . .' she muttered under her breath.

Erika entered the bustling chaos of the school hall for lunch. The unique scent of school dinners drifted through the room: a heady mix of chips, gravy and pizza, with subtle notes of soggy vegetable. Still, nothing could dampen her mood — tonight she was going to have an adventure! Erika grinned as she sat down next to her friend Kris.

'Hey, Erika!' he said. 'I've been making up new jokes, do you want to hear some?'

'Sure thing,' said Erika eagerly. She loved Kris's jokes — he was one of the funniest people she knew.

'OK,' said Kris, adjusting his glasses. 'So, last weekend my mum took me to a cafe that served breakfast at any time.' He paused. 'So we went for sausage and eggs in the Stone Age.'

Erika chuckled as Kris carried on. 'What's brown and sticky?'

'I don't know,' said Erika.

'A stick!' replied Kris. He smiled as she laughed and then pretended to look sad.

'People always point and laugh when I walk the plank – I hope one day my parents actually get me a dog.'

Erika exploded with laughter. When she had calmed down she said to Kris, 'Hey, you should enter the talent show! You'd be brilliant!'

Kris's smile vanished. 'No way. It's one thing telling jokes to you, but what if I was standing up there and got the punchline wrong? What if I just froze? Or worse... what if *nobody laughed*?'

Kris looked so worried at the idea that Erika didn't try to convince him to enter. It was strange though, *everyone* could see how funny and clever Kris was – everyone apart from Kris.

Smudges of darkness crept across the sky while Erika and her family sat together in their living room. Erika was sipping

a mug of hot chocolate, savouring every last velvety drop.

'Right then, Randall,' said Erika's mum once their drinks were finished. 'Time for bed, OK?'

'Sto-weeee?' asked Randall.

'Yes, you can have a story,' replied Erika's dad. 'Which one would you like?'

'Wicka!' shouted Randall.

'What's Wicka?' asked Erika's dad. 'It's not one of those Cakey McCake books is it?' He pulled a face. 'Urgh, if I had my way Cakey would be eaten on page two and that would be the end of it!'

'*Peter!*' hissed Erika's mum, glaring at her husband. 'Randall loves those books.'

'Wicka,' repeated Randall. 'EH-WICKA.'

'Ah, you want *me* to read the story?' said Erika. Randall nodded enthusiastically.

'OK then,' she replied. 'But we've got to get you all washed and clean first.'

She held out her hand and Randall took it.

'Are you sure?' asked Erika's mum.

'Yeah,' replied Erika, 'I'm pretty tired too.' Although all she **actually** wanted to do was start her adventure in the Dreamscape. 'I'll get Randall settled down and then go to bed myself.'

Once Randall was washed, dried and in clean pyjamas, Erika helped him into bed and asked him what story he wanted. Randall grinned happily and held out the book he kept underneath his pillow. Erika smiled as she opened it and started

reading to her younger brother.

'Cakey McCake was the HAPPIEST little cake in all of Cakeland, until one day . . .'

Once Erika had finished the story and Randall was quietly snoring, she crept out of his room to get ready for bed and that night's coming adventure.

CHAPTER 2

One minute Erika had been lying in bed, wondering how long it would take her to get to sleep, and then the next moment she found herself in the **DREAM DEFENDERS'** briefing room, meaning that the answer to her question was, '*not very long at all*'.

'Hi, Erika!' exclaimed Silas, pumping his fist. 'Are you ready for adventure?'

'Hey, Silas,' said Erika, smiling at her friend's enthusiasm. Standing next to Silas was a large man made entirely out of stone. His arms were folded and he leaned wearily against the wall.

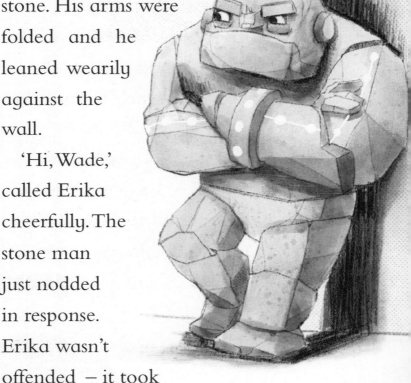

'Hi, Wade,' called Erika cheerfully. The stone man just nodded in response. Erika wasn't offended — it took Wade quite a long time to warm up. No one was sure exactly how long, because they were still waiting for it to happen.

Behind Wade, hopping about from one furry foot to another in barely contained excitement, was Beastling.

'Hi, Beastli—' began Erika, and then she wobbled as Beastling flung all one foot two inches of himself towards her, grabbing her legs in a tight hug.

'Hey, buddy!' She laughed. 'How are you?' Beastling sobbed soggy tears of joy on to her trousers and then finished off by noisily and messily blowing his nose.

He looked up at her and said, '**Heebie**

Jeebie,' in a cracked, broken voice. A speech bubble appeared in the air next to him, showing a misty scene with a plus sign and a lonely sheep. Beastling didn't really speak with words, but instead made speech bubbles with pictures of what he was trying to communicate. Erika stared at the picture, attempting to decipher it.

'Foggy sheep?' she said hesitantly.

'It's easy!' rumbled Wade. 'Mist. Ewe. **Missed you**. See? Even *I* could get that one.'

'Ah!' exclaimed Erika, ruffling the top of Beastling's furry head. 'Of course! Sorry, Beastling.' Erika smiled at her friends. She had missed them, too. It felt great to be back in the Dreamscape with them.

Just then the striking figure of the **DREAM DEFENDERS'** commander Madam Hettyforth appeared, gleaming with a powerful light that shone from within. She was followed almost immediately by a less powerful light as a bedside lamp flickered into view and hopped along the table. As the lamp jumped off the edge it turned into a brightly coloured boy, then a girl, then a boy, and then a girl again. In the end the figure settled on the sleek form of a

jaguar and sat down next to Erika.

'Hi, Erika!' whispered the jaguar.

'Hi, Sim,' replied Erika, smiling at her friend. Sim was a shape-shifter and could transform into anything you could imagine (and even a few things that you probably couldn't!).

'Good. We're all here,' said Madam Hettyforth. 'So, Erika, tonight's subject is Chanda Anand.'

A few images of a
girl a little bit older
than Erika appeared
in the air and Madam
Hettyforth continued. 'Now,
we've been into her dream already, but
to be honest we didn't do very well . . .'

'That wasn't my fault!' interrupted
Sim. 'I was trying to cheer her up by
turning into a giant walking talking ice
cream. I thought it would be funny! How
was I to know that she's scared of ice
cream?'

Erika giggled, but stopped when
Madam Hettyforth looked at her sternly.

'All the same,' said Madam Hettyforth,
'we didn't solve her problem. Erika, I'm
hoping that as another human child

you'll be able to help.'

Erika nodded. 'I'll do my best.'

'I know you will. You always do.' Madam Hettyforth smiled before continuing, 'Chanda's dreams appear to be rebelling against her and, as you'll see, she doesn't even show up on the map of her dream.' Madam Hettyforth tapped at a console and a map of Chanda's dreaming frequency appeared. Sure enough, Chanda's location dot showed up outside the mapped area, in what would ordinarily be a blank void beyond her dream world. Madam Hettyforth frowned. 'It shouldn't even be possible for her to go that far.'

'Show Erika what we got from the Lacunascope,' added Silas.

'Sorry?' interrupted Erika. 'The **what-a-scope?**'

'Lacunascope,' replied Silas. 'It's a device that allows us to look into the subject's day world for short blocks of time. It helps us work out what might be going wrong with their dreams.'

Madam Hettyforth pressed a button and suddenly the

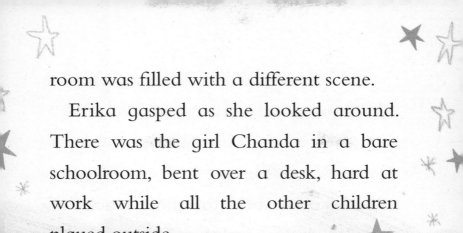

room was filled with a different scene.

Erika gasped as she looked around. There was the girl Chanda in a bare schoolroom, bent over a desk, hard at work while all the other children played outside.

'**WOW** . . .' Erika said softly.

'Pretty cool, right?' asked Sim. Erika nodded, but was distracted as the door to the schoolroom opened and another girl walked in. She strode right through Erika towards Chanda.

'Have you finished?' the girl asked.

'Nearly,' replied Chanda. 'Some of these questions are really hard.'

'Well, yes,' said the girl with a quick laugh. 'But you're so clever! That's why I asked you to help me.' She smiled slightly too brightly before she continued. 'And Chanda?' Chanda looked up as the girl's smile flashed brittle and cold. 'You got a question wrong last week. Make sure that doesn't happen again, OK?'

'Yes, Inu,' replied Chanda, her eyes downcast.

'Anyway, I've got better things to do than hang around waiting for you. Just post the pages at my house on your way home.' Inu's eyes narrowed. 'And remember, **NO MISTAKES**.' She turned to leave without waiting for a reply.

Chanda sighed heavily as she looked back to her work, then the scene flickered and faded to nothing.

'Now, as you can see,' said Madam Hettyforth, 'Chanda's getting pushed around in her waking life. I'm not sure how that relates to what's happening inside her dreams, but there *will* be a connection. First things first, you need to find out where the *woolly-word* Chanda is. Then you can find out what's going wrong in this dream and – finally – solve it. Everybody clear?'

'Yes, Ma'am!' chorused the **DREAM DEFENDERS**.

CHAPTER 3

Countless arches rose high above Erika's head and stretched out far below her, further than she could see. Within each arch there were glowing platforms of light and ranged along each platform were thousands – possibly millions – of doors. They were dream portals, and each one led into a different person's dream.

Right now, Erika and the **DREAM DEFENDERS** were standing outside the door that led into Chanda's dream. Erika was fizzing with the excitement that always came with starting a new adventure.

'Everybody ready?' grunted Wade.

'I was born ready!' said Erika.

'Well, technically you couldn't have been,' replied Silas. 'That would be impossible. A newborn human infant is completely helpless and wouldn't even understand the concept of being "ready", or indeed "not ready".'

Everybody looked at Silas.

'It's just a phrase,' said Erika.

'Oh? Right. Yes, of course it is!' said Silas. 'You humans and your phrases – brilliant, just brilliant!'

'Shall we go and help Chanda now?' asked Wade, glaring at Silas.

'Absolutely!' exclaimed Silas. *I was created-in-a-magical-vortex-from-*

the-memories-of-my-distant-ancestors ready!' He shot a glance over at Erika. 'Did I get that right?'

'Close enough,' said Erika, smiling as they walked through the doorway into Chanda's dream.

They arrived on a hill on the outskirts of a huge, brightly lit town. A rollercoaster twisted across the skyline, shooting high into the air and running through the buildings. The sky gleamed

with a glittering, iridescent light and
extra illumination shone down from
glowing orbs that hung pulsing in the air.

At the centre of the town was a palace
with a huge tower that soared up to

scrape the undersides of the clouds. Water slides cascaded out of the upper floors, and parts of the town were coated in the most picture-perfect snow drifts Erika had ever seen. She sighed with happiness as she gazed out at Chanda's dream – it was beautiful.

But as Erika stared, it became apparent that something wasn't quite right. Dark shadows swam along the lanes of the town and she could just make out some odd creatures scuttling back and forth between the buildings.

'What is that?' asked Erika, pointing down at a large, horned creature that was slithering along one of the streets.

Beastling muttered, **'Heebie Jeebie,'** and made a speech bubble showing a

newspaper covered
in upsetting
headlines.

'It's hard to
say from this distance,'
said Silas. 'I think it's a **Creepator**. But
Beastling's right, it's basically bad news.
It's even worse than when we came here
yesternight. It looks like her dream has
been completely hijacked.'

'Let's not waste any more time then,'
said Wade, peering at a tracking device
on his wrist. 'We need to get to Chanda,
now!' He pointed to a small dot on his
device that was pulsing weakly in the
distance.

With one last look at Chanda's dream-
gone-wrong, Erika turned and followed

the rest of the team as they headed away from the town, towards a thick forest.

After they had walked through the woods for a while, Erika noticed that the trees didn't seem very real. They looked like a toddler's drawing of a tree – scratchy brown lines for the trunks and blobs for the leaves.

'Er, what's going on with the trees?' she asked.

'We're beyond the normal range of the dream now,' explained Silas, 'so the architects don't bother putting in as much detail. Nobody's meant to come out this far.'

As they carried on walking, the trees

became simple poles that stuck up out of the ground. Eventually the trees stopped completely, leaving just a blankness.

'Hey, look! Up ahead!' exclaimed Sim. She was pointing to a tiny, ramshackle hut that was barely visible in the nothingness. Rain was falling above the building and mist clung to the air around it. The whole place seemed desolate and unloved.

'I think we've found Chanda . . .' said Wade as they walked up to the hut and knocked on the stained old door.

Immediately a girl's voice answered, 'I'll be there in a minute! What do you want me to do?'

'Woah! Easy there!' Silas called through the door gently. 'We don't want you to do anything. We're here to help you.'

The door opened slowly and a girl peered out, looking at them disbelievingly. 'You're here to help me?'

Wade rolled his eyes and muttered under his breath, 'We don't have time for this.'

'Shall we use a Full Awareness Blast?' asked Sim.

Erika looked around at the **DREAM DEFENDERS**. 'And that is?'

'Something to help. It'll mean that for the duration of this Dreamcycle Chanda will know that she's dreaming,' explained Silas. 'Basically, she'll be just like you – until she wakes up.'

'What are you talking about?' asked Chanda, looking from face to face. 'I'm sorry, I've got a million and one jobs

to do so if you could—'

Silas looked over at Sim and Wade. 'Shall we?'

They nodded and Silas said, 'Three, two . . . *one*!'

There was an immense flash that left trails in Erika's eyes.

'Whaaa . . .' said Chanda slowly as the light faded. She looked around at them, understanding slowly dawning on her face. 'I'm asleep . . . this a dream, we're in the Dreamscape, you're the **DREAM DEFENDERS**. This is all completely INSANE! And . . .' she looked over at Wade, 'and why are you wearing stone pants?'

'OK,' said Silas, patting Wade on the arm. 'I'll deal with this.

So, just to confirm: yes, yes, yes, yes, yes *and* because otherwise it would be a bit weird. But just going back to point four quickly – you're right, we *are* the **DREAM DEFENDERS** and it's our job to help fix your dream which, as you may or may not have noticed, has gone completely off track.'

As the **DREAM DEFENDERS** walked into the hut Silas added, 'I mean, this cabin doesn't really look very "dreamy" does it?'

Chanda looked around the bare room with its dreary grey walls and one solitary window. She shook her head sadly.

'But that doesn't matter,' cut in Erika, putting her arm round Chanda's shoulder and giving Silas a *what-do-you-think-you're-doing-we're-meant-to-be-helping* sort of look.

'See, that's what the **DREAM DEFENDERS** do! We go in and repair broken dreams. There's not a dream that we can't fix. Right, team?'

'Actually...' began Sim, 'there was that boy's dream where elephants kept falling out of the sky and squashing his pets. We never did get to the bottom of—'

'*There's not a dream we can't fix!*' repeated Erika, giving Sim the same look she had just given Silas.

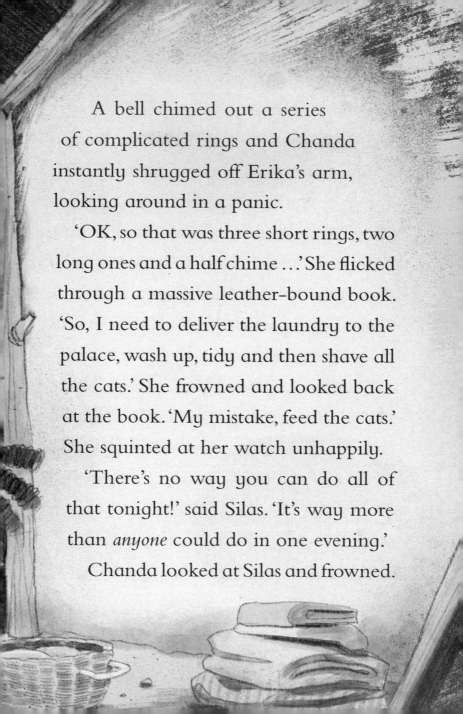

A bell chimed out a series of complicated rings and Chanda instantly shrugged off Erika's arm, looking around in a panic.

'OK, so that was three short rings, two long ones and a half chime ...' She flicked through a massive leather-bound book. 'So, I need to deliver the laundry to the palace, wash up, tidy and then shave all the cats.' She frowned and looked back at the book. 'My mistake, feed the cats.' She squinted at her watch unhappily.

'There's no way you can do all of that tonight!' said Silas. 'It's way more than *anyone* could do in one evening.'

Chanda looked at Silas and frowned.

'That's my list of jobs for the next *hour*.'

'No,' said Erika, 'it's not! Whoever's stolen your dream is about to have a nasty surprise! You're going to **STOP** doing everything for them. They don't know it yet, but they're about to come up against something **SO** powerful they couldn't even imagine it!'

Sim's eyes gleamed. 'Oooh, that sounds amazing! What is it?'

Beastling grinned and said, 'Heebie Jeebie,' creating a picture of the DREAM DEFENDERS standing in various heroic poses. 'Oh, yeah, right! Of course!'

said Sim, looking embarrassed. 'Silly me.'

'So, what do we know for certain?' asked Sim, who had taken on the form of a schoolteacher and was pacing up and down Chanda's hut, glancing around. 'Any ideas? Erika? Silas? Wade?'

'Well, we know the dream's been overrun with monsters,' said Erika. 'But what are they all doing here?'

'Someone – or something –

must be bringing them here,' said Silas. 'None of these monsters are clever enough to organize something like this on their own. There's got to be *something* pulling the strings.'

Sim nodded sagely. 'There was a concentration of creatures around the palace at the centre of the town. I'm willing to bet that we'll get the answers we're looking for in there.'

Wade tapped the buttons on his wrist and then frowned. 'Weird . . .' he murmured. 'I tried to take a look inside the palace but whatever's in there has managed to screen off the whole building. I can't get any information — look.' He tapped his wrist again and the diagram of the palace appeared in mid-air.

'I don't understand,' said Erika. 'We can see the whole thing.'

'But look,' continued Wade. 'It's empty. Ordinarily I'd be able to see whoever was inside, but something is blocking it.'

'So, we've got no idea what we're up against?' asked Chanda.

'I'm afraid not,' said Silas. 'But that's all part of the fun, right?'

Chanda did not look so sure.

'OK!' said Wade decisively. 'So, basically, we need to fight our way inside the palace, find out what's disrupting Chanda's dream and crush it!' He pounded one giant fist into the other. 'Then we can take control of this dream frequency and pass it back over to Chanda. Agreed?'

They all hesitated.

'Yeah, I guess so . . .' said Sim finally.

'I don't know.' Chanda sounded nervous. 'I mean, I suppose I do need your help, but that all sounds a bit, well, you know . . . *fight-y!*'

Beastling nodded and whispered, '**Heebie Jeebie**,' creating a picture of Wade getting into a fight and looking really happy about it.

'*Nonsense!*' growled Wade. 'It's the fastest way to deal with the problem. Look, sometimes you just have to act! So, let's get out there and get this dream back!' He paused for a moment and looked expectantly around the group.

'OK ...' said Silas slowly. 'Chanda, when we get into town, you stay close to Erika and me – we'll make sure you're safe.'

Chanda's silent nod didn't help Erika feel any better about what they were about to do.

'I thought that was a pretty good motivational speech,' muttered Wade. 'But nobody even whooped or cheered or *anything*.'

CHAPTER 4

'Remember, it's *essential* that we get inside without being spotted,' said Silas. 'At least, it is if we want to avoid a full-scale battle!'

Wade looked slightly disappointed but nodded his agreement.

They were all creeping through the deserted streets of Chanda's dream town, heading for the palace. It was quite hard for Erika to creep though, because Beastling had decided that this was the ideal time to take a nap

and was curled up inside her backpack, along with a wide selection of snacks in case he got hungry mid-snooze.

As they approached a crossroads Wade stopped abruptly, held up four fingers on his left hand and moved it slowly round in a circle. Everyone stared at him with blank expressions and he sighed heavily. 'Just be careful!' he whispered. 'We have three enemies ahead.'

Erika peered around the corner and saw a huge building with a sign that had:

EXQUISITE MEMORY EMPORIUM

painted on it in shiny metallic letters. In the windows of the shop were hundreds of paintings, television screens and monitors. Each one showed a different happy memory of Chanda's. One large, gilt frame held an animated painting of Chanda finding an injured bird and nursing it back to health. Nearby, an old-fashioned television showed a black-and-white clip of her winning an award for schoolwork, while everyone around her clapped. But creeping around in the shop were four mean-looking **Hornheads**.

'My fifth birthday!' whispered Chanda, happily. She pointed to a television that showed a younger version of herself with her family, all running along a beach of black sand into the sea.

'That sand was so hot!' she added. 'I couldn't wait to get into the sea!' She smiled so broadly that it made Erika smile, too.

Then one of the **Hornheads** in the shop went up to the television and kicked it. Now it showed a clip of a young Chanda tripping over in the playground and hurting her knee.

Soon, all the screens and paintings showed unhappy, troubling scenes.

Erika's heart sank as she heard Chanda whisper, 'My happy memories ... I'm losing them, I can feel them all fading away ...'

Erika felt a familiar heat rising up through her. She gritted her teeth, and before she knew it, she was about to run out and confront the creatures who were ruining Chanda's dream.

'*No!*' hissed Silas, grabbing her arm. 'Not like that! We *will* stop them, but we've got to be sensible. If you just rush out like this then we blow it all. OK?'

Erika looked at her friend and took a deep breath, then she nodded.

When the coast was clear, they crept on again.

Each road in the town had been named after something important to Chanda, but all the signs had been yanked off the walls or painted over. The feeling was echoed wherever they went – the whole happy world had been distorted into something cold, dark and bitter.

Erika turned to face Chanda. 'Don't worry,' she said. She was pained to see how dejected her friend looked. 'We'll get this fixed. I promise we will!'

'How do we get inside the palace?' asked Silas. 'It's one thing sneaking around a few **Hornheads**, but there are **Dragon Whales** up there!' He pointed into the sky where four huge shapes circled through the air around the main

palace tower. Their massive bulk seemed
too large to be held up by their delicate
wings, but somehow they stayed in the
air. Dangerous, sharp-toothed mouths
flickered and sparked with electric power
as they periodically spat bolts of lightning

down to the ground.

'Yeah. We probably can't just go and knock on the door,' said Sim.

'Do you think there's a more hidden route?' asked Erika, her eyes wide as she gazed at up the awe-inspiring creatures.

'Well, there's the tunnel I use to take back all the ironed socks,' said Chanda. 'There's hardly ever anyone down there.'

'Fantastic!' replied Wade. 'That'll be our way in!'

* * * * *

Light flickered from the torch that Wade held in front of them as they walked in single file down the narrow tunnel.

'How long is this going to take?' muttered the torch. 'And can you stop holding me so tightly, it's pinching!'

'Be quiet, Sim!' hissed Wade.

'Shhh, all of you!' said Silas. 'There's something ahead.'

Erika peered through the gloom to see a thick, heavy-looking door. It was locked and bolted with a chain

that was secured by a huge padlock.

'Hmm,' said Chanda, 'that padlock wasn't there before . . .'

'Don't worry,' said Erika, 'we've got Wade. He can just smash that padlock off and we'll be inside.'

'Maybe not,' replied Silas uneasily. 'That's a Padmad — a Dreamscape monster that takes the shape of a lock. You have to try to convince it to open very carefully or it will go berserk. It's like a lock and alarm system all in one. Plus they've got really sharp teeth.'

Erika peered closely at the Padmad, and it peered back at her.

'So what do we do?' she asked.

'We say nice things to it,' said Sim. 'Padmads are suspicious of strangers and will only ever open for a trusted friend, so we need to win it around. Like this.' She changed back into her usual form, bent down so that her face was close to the Padmad and cooed, 'Hey there, little fella, how's it going? It must get lonely down here in the cold and the dark?'

'ME LIKE THE DARK!' hissed the Padmad.

'Yes, *yes*, of course you do!' continued Sim soothingly. 'And what a great door to guard. You must be *very* important.'

'**YES,**' replied the monster, sounding proud of itself. '**PADMAD BRAVE, TOO.**'

'Of *course!*' replied Sim. 'Only someone incredibly brave could do such a difficult and dangerous job. I bet your locking mechanism is *very* complicated.'

'**VERY!**' The Padmad looked like it was trying to nod – if padlocks could nod.

'Could you show me how it works?' asked Sim. 'Just a tiny bit—'

'**YOU NOT TRICK ME!**' growled the Padmad.

'Oh *no!*' said Sim, sounding genuinely wounded. 'I would **never** try to trick you. I just love seeing how complicated things work.'

'**I SHOW YOU A BIT . . .**' replied the Padmad. As it spoke the whole door started to shift and change. The individual planks of wood slid around and rotated like a huge, three-dimensional puzzle.

Erika and Chanda stared at the Padmad in amazement.

'It's not just the padlock,' explained Silas. 'It's the whole door. They're not the brightest creatures in the Dreamscape, but they're certainly a good design!'

Now we just need to wait for Sim to get it *completely* on side and we can—'

'We haven't got time for this!' grunted Wade as he shoved a rock into the mechanism. 'Let's just jam it open!'

'Wade!' protested Sim. 'I was nearly there—' But she was cut off by a furious shrieking. The Padmad's angry howl rang and reverberated down the tunnel, until even the echoes of the echoes had echoes. **'ENEMY! ENEMY! ENEMY!'** it wailed relentlessly.

A throbbing pain beat in Erika's eardrums, even though she had her hands pressed tightly to her head.

As soon as Wade had the door open he shouted, 'LET'S GO!' But the words were barely audible over the noise of the Padmad. They climbed through the gap into the main castle and seconds later were sprinting away from the hideous sound.

'What did you do *that* for Wade?' asked Silas, as they darted up a spiral staircase. They were well away from the Padmad now but could still hear it shrieking away below them.

'We're inside the palace aren't we?' grumbled Wade.

'Yes,' agreed Silas, 'but now every

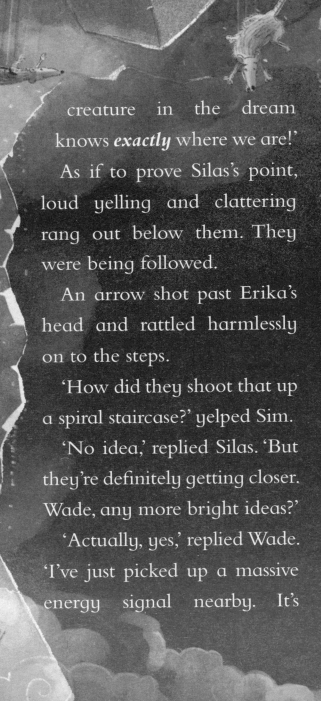

creature in the dream knows *exactly* where we are!'

As if to prove Silas's point, loud yelling and clattering rang out below them. They were being followed.

An arrow shot past Erika's head and rattled harmlessly on to the steps.

'How did they shoot that up a spiral staircase?' yelped Sim.

'No idea,' replied Silas. 'But they're definitely getting closer. Wade, any more bright ideas?'

'Actually, yes,' replied Wade. 'I've just picked up a massive energy signal nearby. It's weird, there was nothing there a second ago. Let's check it out.'

He suddenly stopped running and everyone else collided with him. Sim nearly tumbled backwards down the stairs.

Wade pressed his hands to the wall and frowned with exertion. The stone blocks spun and ground themselves around into a different formation. Seconds later they weren't looking at a blank wall – there was a jagged tunnel entrance instead. Dust, spiders and a few surprised rats fell down as Wade created more of the tunnel.

The noises coming up the staircase were getting louder and louder. Wade turned and closed up the wall behind them, just as their pursuers appeared round the corner.

'It's directly this way,' grunted Wade, ignoring the muffled shouting on the other side of the wall. 'Shouldn't take long to get there.'

His tunnelling increased in intensity until he was almost flinging the stones aside and huge billowing clouds of dust were rising up all around them. Erika gasped as she found herself stumbling forwards through a hole in a wall and collapsing in a dusty heap on the floor.

As her vision cleared, Erika looked round the lavish room they were in. She was sprawled on the floor behind a huge, ornate throne.

'Is everyone all right?' asked Erika. Wade, Sim and Silas nodded grimly, getting slowly to their feet. The only person who didn't respond was Chanda. Erika looked up to see her new friend walking slowly out of view round the side of the throne.

'What is it?' whispered Erika.

'What is it? How rude!' called out Chanda.

At least, it sounded like Chanda, but stronger, more self-assured and colder – as though every ounce of warmth and kindness had been stripped away. 'Why don't you come and see for yourself?'

Erika's legs quivered beneath her.

What was going on?

'Well, come on!' called the voice. 'I can't bear the anticipation!'

Erika peered round the side of the throne and stopped short. Her eyes widened.

Sitting in the chair, a terrible mocking smile on her cruel lips, was Chanda.

CHAPTER 5

Erika looked round in confusion. There was Chanda, looking horrified and bewildered by the side of the throne, but there she also was *on* the throne – imperious, strong and completely at ease.

'A **DOUBT!**' whispered Silas.

'A *what*?' asked Erika.

'Oh, *really*?' intoned the figure on the throne with a mock shudder. 'Must you? I loathe that term, so uninspiring! I mean, do I look **DOUBTY**? Hardly!

If anything, she's the one that should be called a **DOUBT**.' It shot a scornful glance towards Chanda. 'I mean, look at her! The poor thing can hardly bear to look at me!'

'What . . . what *are* you?' asked Chanda, her voice trembling.

The **DOUBT** laughed. 'Come on, Chanda!

You're going to have to do a lot better than that. I can't believe I was ever a part of you!'

Silas shook his head sadly. 'That's what **DOUBTS** always do,' he muttered. 'They start off as a quiet voice in the back of your head, whispering negative things, and if they're left unchecked they become so overpowering that they split off and become independent of the dreamer. I can't believe we didn't think of that before.'

Erika looked at him. 'So . . . how do we beat it?'

'We can't!' replied Silas. 'Only the dreamer can defeat their own **DOUBT**. That's why they're so dangerous!'

Without any warning, Wade spun round and sent a massive tidal wave of vibration shooting through the flagstone floor. The throne crashed to the ground, breaking into hundreds of pieces, and tapestries on the wall billowed and danced in clouds of dust.

'And what exactly were you hoping

to achieve by doing that?' asked a voice from the middle of the carnage. The dust cleared to reveal the **DOUBT**, standing

completely untouched. 'You can't physically harm me! I'm going to just keep getting stronger and stronger while she –' the **DOUBT** stared unblinkingly at Chanda – 'gets even weaker. By the end of the next Dreamcycle I will have enough power to completely take over. There won't even be a Chanda any more and then I can control her waking life as well!'

'No!' gasped Chanda.

The **DOUBT** laughed. 'Yes. Now, this little chat has been tremendous fun, but I'm getting bored.' The **DOUBT** waved its hand and a massive hole suddenly opened up in the floor beneath the **DREAM DEFENDERS**. Seconds later they were falling down the stone chutes into complete darkness!

Erika landed hard. She gasped as the wind was knocked out of her and lay still on the floor trying to get her breath back. They were in some sort of large

stone chamber, with a compressed earth floor that was scattered with bones. There was no way in or out, apart from the chute in the ceiling that they had just fallen through.

Large hands roughly grabbed Erika and heaved her to her feet. 'We need to get out of here, and quickly,' grunted Wade. 'I don't like this one bit!'

As Wade spoke, the floor began to shift beneath Erika's feet. She almost tripped over a bone as it burrowed upwards out of the earth and rolled sideways along the ground, connecting to a nearby skull with an ominous click.

'What was *that*?' shrieked Erika, her pulse quickening. Dozens of bones were now bouncing and rolling towards each other across the churning ground, connecting together in a chaotic way.

The trickle bouncing past Erika became a stream, then a river, until a roaring torrent of skeletal debris was towering above them like a tidal wave.

'A **Bone Cobble!**' gasped Sim.

Wade heaved a massive block out of the wall and hurled it at the creature's head, but all the individual bones moved slightly and the stone passed straight through it. Sim morphed into a sabre-toothed tiger and leaped forwards, trying to grab whatever bones she could from the mess of the creature, while Silas fired blinding flares of light up towards its face. Nothing made any difference. The creature kept coming.

'**SHOCKWAVES!**' shouted Wade. 'Everybody stand back!' Kneeling down, he started pounding the floor with his massive fists. The earth shook, slowly at

first, then faster and faster, until Erika's vision shook, too. It felt as though the whole world was vibrating. She could

barely keep her feet. The pounding increased to an unbearable level as Silas yelled, 'It's working!'

The **Bone Cobble** was losing its form — teeth, ribs, skulls and lots of other unidentifiable bits of bone were raining down to the ground. Soon, all that remained was just a mound of bits and pieces. Wade stopped pounding the ground and stood up slowly, rubbing his back and arms.

'Yes!' yelled Erika. 'Well done, Wade!'

'Wait!' gasped Chanda, pointing at the bones that were already rolling and bouncing towards each other again — the **Bone Cobble** was reforming!

The **DREAM DEFENDERS** looked at each other.

'So, what now?' whispered Erika.

'It depends,' grunted Wade. 'Do you want to be eaten, killed or taken prisoner by that **DOUBT**?'

'Er, none of the above?' replied Erika.

'No. Me neither,' said Wade. 'So we need to abort the mission and reconsider our options in a safer environment.'

'You mean, give up and run away?' cried Erika. 'But what about Chanda? We can't just leave her here like this!'

'What do *you* suggest we do?' retorted Wade. 'It's nearly the end of Chanda's Dreamcycle. Any second now she's going to wake up and vanish. So *yes*, Erika, I say we abort the mission and reconsider our options.'

Erika scowled. 'But we can't just abandon—'

'Erika,' said Chanda, touching her on the arm. 'It's OK. I know that you

want to help, but seriously, take a look
around . . .' She gestured to the bones
that were wriggling towards each other
as the **Bone Cobble** grew larger by the
second. 'You really need to get out of here!
And don't worry about me.' She smiled.
'I mean, it's typical really — trust me to
have a hard time, even in my dreams!'

Just as she said those words, Chanda
flickered and vanished.

'Chanda?' called Erika. '*Chanda!*'

'Don't worry,' said Silas. 'She's just

woken up. She'll be fine. But we won't if we hang around! Come on, let's get out of here. We can fix this tomorrow night, I promise!'

'HQ! This is squad 077,' yelled Wade, pressing the communication device on his wrist. 'Requesting **EMERGENCY** evacuation.' He frowned so hard that bits of gravel chipped off his forehead. 'What do you mean, "*when*"? I mean NOW! Was the word **EMERGENCY** not clear enough?'

The **Bone Cobble** towered above Erika, rising up into a mountain of bones. Shrieking and screaming furiously, the multitude of skulls dived down, striking the floor at exactly the same moment the **DREAM DEFENDERS** vanished.

The next thing Erika knew she was back at **DREAM DEFENDERS** HQ. The formidable figure of Madam Hettyforth was towering over them, hands on hips and an expression on her face somewhere between *incredibly angry* and *completely furious*.

'Wade McRubble!' she barked. 'Watching you thundering around in there was like watching a dog trying to order pizza over the telephone! Do you

have *anything* to say for yourself?'

Wade did not have a lot to say for himself. Or rather, he didn't have a lot to say that made any difference to Madam Hettyforth's mood. The more he spoke, the crosser she got, and so after a while he just fell silent.

'What a disaster!' tutted Madam Hettyforth. 'A complete waste of a Dreamcycle.'

'But we tried our best!' protested Erika, ignoring the *you-shoud-really-stop-talking* looks that Silas was giving her.

'*Did you?*' asked Madam Hettyforth, frowning. 'That was your *very* best was it?' She inspected the group, who somehow all managed to find somewhere else to look. All except Erika.

'Well, maybe not our *very* best . . .' conceded Erika. 'But given the surprise we had when we discovered the **DOUBT**, I think we did pretty well!'

Madam Hettyforth sighed heavily and shook her head. 'I'm sorry, I'm just frustrated,' she said. 'I've seen too many **DOUBTS** ruin too many dreams. Too many lives . . . We'll just have to work harder next time. Remember what's at stake here!'

'I know,' said Silas. 'Don't worry, Ma'am, we'll think of something.'

'I hope so . . .' said Madam Hettyforth. 'Now, Erika, will you be able to help again next Dreamcycle? It seemed like Chanda really connected with you.'

'Yes!' replied Erika. 'Of course.'

Madam Hettyforth looked round at the group once more. 'OK. Well, that's settled then. Sim, you take Erika back to her own dream and then tomorrow's another night.'

CHAPTER 6

Erika woke up back in her bed at home. She lay there for a moment, feeling bad about what had happened – the **DREAM DEFENDERS** had failed Chanda. There was just one more chance to get things right tonight, and in the meantime she had a whole day of school to get through.

Erika was feeling very distracted as she got ready, and was about to leave the house when her mum pointed out that she was wearing her jumper back to front.

Throughout the day, that sort of thing kept happening. She walked into the wrong classroom and sat down with the tiny reception kids without even realizing. She accidentally put her coat on the wrong hook and accused Sally Jenkins of hiding it. Instead of bringing all her schoolbooks she had picked up a pile of old books her dad was taking to the charity shop and opened *Binky and Fluffkins Go to the Beach* in the middle of her maths lesson.

All she could think about was Chanda. *How was she feeling? Was that girl Inu being mean again? Would the* **DREAM DEFENDERS** *be able to get rid of the* **DOUBT***?*

It was strange; the day felt the wrong way round, like her waking life was a distraction from her important work with the **DREAM DEFENDERS**.

At lunchtime Erika did the only thing she could think of — she went to visit the school library to do some research. She trawled the shelves, collecting all the books she could find on dreams and what they mean, but none of it was much help. Unless you wanted to know what it meant if you dreamed that your teeth fell out (you were worried about money, apparently).

She was so focused on her books, a deep frown furrowing her eyebrows, that she didn't notice Kris walking over to her.

'Hi, Erika!' he said brightly.

'Oh, hi, Kris,' replied Erika, glancing up and rubbing her eyes.

'Are you OK?' asked Kris.

'What?' said Erika distractedly. 'Yeah, great . . .'

'It's just that you were sat like this.' Kris twisted his body up and hunched over a book with an expression of exaggerated concern on his face.

'Ha!' Erika laughed out loud. 'Was I? Well . . . I've got this problem I need to solve.'

'What is it?' asked Kris, sitting down next

to her. 'Maybe I can help?'

Erika frowned again. Kris was a good friend and she knew she could trust him, but the **DREAM DEFENDERS** had to be kept completely secret. She decided she *could* tell Kris what the problem was, as long as she didn't mention the **DREAM DEFENDERS**. She thought for a moment.

'OK . . .' she said eventually. 'Well, I have this friend who just doesn't seem to realize how awesome they are. You know, clever, funny and, deep down, brave. I really want to help, but I just can't figure out how!' Kris went quiet and looked over at Erika, an unusually serious expression on his face.

'Right,' he said slowly. 'Well, it sounds to me like your "friend" –' he made air quotes with his fingers – 'needs to find a way to feel a bit more confident about themself.'

Erika looked at him, a grin slowly spreading on her face. 'Yes! That's exactly it. Thanks, Kris!'

The bell rang for the end of lunch and Erika leaped up to go back to class, not noticing how thoughtful Kris seemed.

* ✶ ✶ ✶ ✶

The afternoon passed uneventfully, apart from when Erika accidentally set off the school fire alarm by leaning against it while she was thinking about Chanda. Then she got her school bag caught in a bus door at the end of the day, except she hadn't realized it was actually Sally Jenkins' bag – which was now all crushed up and door-mashed. So before she went home she had to walk to Sally's house to give it back and apologize for the state it was in, *plus* she had to try and explain that she hadn't taken it on purpose. So, actually, it had been quite an eventful afternoon.

All in all, Erika was glad to finally get home and shut the door on the rest of the day.

She trudged into the kitchen and slung her bag down on the floor.

'Are you all right, love?' asked Erika's mum.

'Urgh, yeah, I guess,' replied Erika, getting a glass of squash.

'Are you sure?' asked her dad, raising his eyebrows. 'It's just that you're drinking a glass of diluted vinegar.'

Erika spat out the liquid in her mouth. *Who would put the vinegar next to the squash bottles?*

She quickly rinsed her mouth out with water and then said, 'No, I'm fine. It's just been one of those days.'

'I've been having one of those weeks!' said Erika's mum.

'I'm having one of those lives!' added Erika's dad. 'Anyway, who fancies watching some TV and a nice, hot cup of vinegar?' He winked at Erika, who grinned back.

'Oooh, yes,' said Erika's mum. 'Two salts in mine, please.'

Randall smiled happily and waved his sippy cup around in the air to join in.

Erika smiled. Her parents were total goofs, but somehow they always seemed to be able to cheer her up.

By the time Erika went to bed later that evening she was in a much better mood. She smiled as she climbed under the duvet. At least she had a plan now – they just had to find a way to build Chanda's confidence.

CHAPTER 7

Back in the Dreamscape that night, Erika and the **DREAM DEFENDERS** walked towards Chanda's hut.

'So, you remember what to do?' said Erika. 'We need to make Chanda feel good about herself. OK?'

Everybody nodded and Erika knocked on the door. Chanda opened it slowly, peering cautiously out.

'Hiya!' said Silas cheerily. 'We were here yesternight. You don't remember us, but you will ... Three, two ... one!' There was a sudden flash of energy as he fired off the dazzling force of the Full Awareness Blast.

'Whaaa . . .' said Chanda slowly. Then she gasped. 'I'm asleep! You're the **DREAM DEFENDERS** and you're trying to help me!' She looked over at Wade. 'But why are you wearing stone pants?'

'Actually,' said Silas, 'we covered that last point before. Don't you remember?'

Chanda frowned. 'Oh yes . . . I *do* remember now – I remember everything!' Her face fell as the events of the previous night came back to her. 'I remember the **DOUBT**,' she said quietly.

'Don't worry about that now!' said Erika hastily.

'Er, Chanda – you have nice ears,' blurted Wade suddenly.

'*What?*' said Chanda and Erika at the same time.

'Your ears,' repeated Wade sounding flustered. 'They're really good ones.'

'Okaaaaay . . .' said Chanda, looking at Wade with confusion. 'Er, thanks. So, what's your plan? How do we reclaim my dream?'

'We've got a few ideas,' said Sim. 'But none as good as the ideas that you'd come up with I'm sure, you're SO smart!'

'Right,' said Chanda. 'Thanks, I guess.'

'**Heebie Jeebie**!' chimed in Beastling, making a picture of Chanda standing on top of a mountain triumphantly, with bright rays of sunshine radiating out around her.

'Er, I'm not entirely sure what you mean.' Chanda was starting to look seriously confused.

'He's basically saying you're **AMANZING**,' said Silas. 'Which you are! Can you sing? I bet you can! You look like you could sing really well.'

'What do good singers look like?' asked Chanda, frowning in confusion.

'Er . . .' said Silas.

'OK. What's going on?' demanded Chanda. 'Why are you all being weird?'

Wade, Silas, Sim and Erika looked at each other. Nobody said anything. Then Erika sighed. 'They're trying to boost your confidence,' she said. 'Saying nice things to try to make you feel good about yourself.'

'Is that how you see me?' Chanda asked quietly. 'With no confidence?'

'No,' said Erika, reaching out to touch her friend on the arm. 'I just thought that maybe you needed a bit of help to see yourself how *we* see you.'

'Well, thanks for trying,' said Chanda,

flashing a weak smile. 'But just as a note, Wade, literally nobody in the history of EVER has even once tried to compliment someone on their ears.'

'I *was* going to say you had an effective digestive system,' muttered Wade, 'but *Erika* said that would have been weird.'

'And she was right,' said Chanda. 'So, anyway, what now? How are we going to get my dream back?'

'Let's try something else,' said Erika. 'I want you to say something that you like about yourself. You know, something you feel proud of. If it was me, I might say, "I always try to help my friends". Do you get it?'

'I'll give it a go,' said Chanda. She frowned for a moment and then paused and frowned even harder. After another pause she said, 'I can't.'

'It could be *anything*,' encouraged Erika.

'I can't do it!' said Chanda desperately. 'I literally can't say anything good about myself. My head's just full of bad thoughts!'

'Can **DOUBTS** actually do that?' asked Erika. 'Stop people from thinking good things about themselves?'

'I'm afraid so,' said Silas quietly.

'Right!' exclaimed Erika. 'We're going to silence that **DOUBT** once and for all!'

'Absolutely!' said Silas very enthusiastically. 'But ... you do remember what happened last time, right? It didn't go so well.'

'Yes,' said Erika, 'but last time I hadn't just come up with a BRILLIANT plan! Now, here's what we're going to do . . .'

CHAPTER 8

THUD! THUD! THUD!

Heavy bone knuckles slammed against the palace door as a massive, filthy **Bone Cobble** loomed over the entrance. It was completely covered in dust from head to toe even though, being a **Bone Cobble**, it had more than one head and approximately twenty-five thousand toes.

A grate slid back on the door, revealing the sentry's suspicious eyes.

'Who's there?'

'PRISONERS!' intoned a deep,

rumbling voice from somewhere inside the mass of bones. Behind the **Bone Cobble** the streets were still filled with dreadful creatures, skulking around and laughing as they vandalized the buildings in Chanda's dream town.

The eyes behind the grate widened excitedly as they fell upon Erika, Beastling, Chanda, Wade and Silas.

'Let me go!' hissed Erika, struggling against the crushing bone tentacles that bound them.

'Oh, I don't think so,' replied the sentry. 'Now, come on – get them inside!' The screen slammed shut and, with an ear-piercing squeak, the door creaked open.

'*Yeeesh*,' muttered the **Bone Cobble**, wincing. 'You should really get some oil on that.'

'I keep saying that,' replied the sentry, 'but, oh no, the boss likes it. Says it adds "mood", says it adds "atmosphere". I say it gives a bad impress—Wait . . . I've never heard one of you lot ever speak more than two words at a time.'

'Uh, PRACTISING,' rumbled the **Bone Cobble** hesitantly.

'Well, good for you!' said the sentry, swishing her large tail across the floor. 'It's always good to try new things. I did a skydive last year. Now, you get these prisoners inside and go off to be creepy somewhere else. The castle guards will take them from here.'

'Er, ME TAKE PRISONERS!' replied the **Bone Cobble**.

'I do *not* think so!' said the sentry, putting her hands on her hips. 'You're filthy! Can't have trails of muck all through the palace, can we?' She turned to rummage around in a store cupboard. 'Now, where did I put those restraints?'

Chanda's pale, round eyes darted nervously around the room before resting on Erika.

'It'll be all right,' Erika whispered. 'At least . . . it usually is.'

'There, found them!' called the sentry cheerily, carrying five sets of what looked like handcuffs.

'Right, pass me the shadow one first.'

Slowly the bone tentacles clicked and clattered around, releasing Silas from their suffocating grip. The sentry held out the manacles and clamped them around his wrists.

'Right, let's do the human dreamer next I think.' Chanda looked at Erika, desperation drawn on every inch of her face.

'No!' yelled Erika. **'STOP!** You can't do this!'

'You really should have thought about that before you burst in here and started interfering in our business! And just in case you get any funny ideas . . . ' The sentry pulled an alarm cord on the wall and seconds later the room was filled with guards.

The **Bone Cobble** looked nervously around.

'ME GO NOW,' it rumbled uncertainly.

'Oh no. I think you should stay,' said the sentry. 'After all, you can't abandon your friends, can you?'

'What!' gasped the **Bone Cobble**. 'How did you know?'

The sentry raised an eyebrow and pointed to a brightly coloured patch of bone where the dust and dirt had been rubbed off.

'You don't often see a **Bone Cobble** *that* colour!'

Sim gasped.

'And don't even think about trying to get away,' added the sentry. 'That alarm summoned every creature we have in our army. You're quite literally surrounded.'

Moving quickly, the **Bone Cobble** released Erika, Chanda, Beastling and Wade, helping them back out of the door as it swung a bony tentacle towards the guards, knocking a few of them off their feet.

Erika grabbed Chanda's hand and turned to run. They forced their way past a few guards, but then came up against a huge mass of creatures approaching the palace – there were

just too many. The sentry was right, they were surrounded!

Sim changed from the **Bone Cobble** into a dragon and tried to swoop down to grab the rest of the **DREAM DEFENDERS** but there were too many enemies around them. She couldn't even shoot out her fiery breath in case she accidentally hit her friends.

'GO!' yelled Wade. 'We'll be OK, it's no use all of us getting captured.'

Sim's eyes danced across from one to another of her friends.

'Now!' shrieked Erika. 'Go on! Get out of here!'

Finally, with one last desperate look at them, Sim fled.

CHAPTER 9

Erika sat on the cold, hard floor of a stone cell. Beastling was sitting on her lap, nestling into her for comfort. Since they'd found themselves locked in there more than two hours ago, Chanda hadn't said a single word. She hadn't even looked at anyone. Erika and the others had tried everything they could think of to escape, but there was something in the cell that rendered their skills useless.

Wade couldn't make a single stone vibrate, let alone break down a wall. He pounded at the door with his huge fists, but it didn't move a millimetre.

They were stuck.

'Hey, Chanda,' said Erika. '*Chanda!*' But the girl didn't respond. She just sat slumped against the wall, arms on her knees, her head hanging low. Wade, Beastling, Silas and Erika glanced at each other.

'Look, don't worry,' said Erika, 'we'll find a way out. We just have to keep trying, OK? Never give up, right?'

Chanda completely ignored her.

'Tough crowd,' said Silas quietly. He tried to use his powers of manipulation to convince the guard on the other side of the door to let them go, but it didn't work. The guard just opened up the grate and laughed in his face.

'Look, I know what you're trying to do, and it won't work. This cell has been fully prepared against any attempt to escape from within. Your powers won't work in it. *YOU'RE COMPLETELY TRAPPED!*' He pressed his face up closer to the small hatch in the door and peered around. 'Hey, you! Dreamer.'

Chanda turned her head slowly around and looked at the guard with sad, heavy eyes.

'I'm enjoying your dream castle!' The guard laughed. 'Thanks for letting us have it!' Then he slammed the grate shut, although the muffled sound of laughter continued.

'Don't listen to him!' said Erika quickly. 'We'll find a way out. Look, all we need to do is come up with a plan—'

'What's the point?' interrupted Chanda. 'Whatever it is, it's not going to work! That *thing* up there in the throne room is going to win. It'll take over my life and what then? I'll be trapped here in this weird dream world and I'll never see my family again. I'll never wake up.'

A small, brightly coloured spider sniffled as it descended slowly toward Erika from the ceiling.

'That is the saddest thing I have ever heard!' it said. 'If only there was some sort of rescue party coming to get you out of here. Well, I say rescue party, can you have a party of one person? I don't think you can. I tried to give myself a surprise birthday party once, but it didn't really work. You know, it's REALLY hard to surprise yourself!'

'Sim!' exclaimed Erika. 'You found us!

'Yep!' replied Sim. 'And it took me *aaaaaaages!* I had to stay teeny tiny so I didn't get seen. Have you ever tried to walk down a really long tunnel while you're a woodlouse? Boy, is it *tiring*! Anyway, I'll just change into something massive and break down the door. I'm surprised you didn't try that already, Wade. Anyway, stand back.'

There was a pause and the spider made a quiet grunting sound.

'That's weird. I'm stuck.'

'Oh, really?' asked Wade, smirking. 'Do you want to try again?'

The spider grunted a bit louder.

'Nope,' it gasped. 'It's no good, I can't do it. I've lost my powers! **I'M GOING TO BE A SPIDER FOR THE REST OF MY LIFE.** I'll have to eat flies and live in a horrible dirty web. It's going to be awful!'

'Don't panic,' said Erika. 'The cell has some sort of protection on it. None of us can do anything from inside it. I'm sure you'll be fine once you're outside though.' She paused. '*Wait!* I have an idea, climb on to my hand, Sim.'

Erika knocked on the grate and positioned her hand near it as the grill was sharply opened.

'What?' grunted the guard from outside.

'Hi!' said Erika, smiling broadly.

'What do you want?' asked the guard, his brows knitting tightly together.

'Oh, well, I was just wondering what animal you were most scared of?' asked Erika.

'Hmm, tricky,' muttered the guard, curious despite himself. 'I mean, bears and lions are pretty scary, but overall I think it's got to be a shark.'

'Is a shark an animal?' asked Silas. 'They're fish, aren't they?'

'I don't think it *really* matters right now,' said Erika. 'OK, Sim – *go*!'

The spider leaped off Erika's hand and out through the grate. Seconds later there was a wet, flopping sound and a terrified scream.

Beastling peered through the small hatch and whispered, '**Heebie Jeebie**,' in quiet tones of awe and surprise. Then the door was ripped off its hinges and Erika could see a large, great white shark standing upright on its tail with a chunk of door in its mouth.

'OK,' said Silas, 'that's one of the

weirdest things I've ever seen, and I once saw Wade practising yoga.'

Wade glared at Silas. 'It's actually very good for my stress levels,' he growled as he stomped out across the broken door.

'He's right though Sim, it is a bit distracting. Can you turn back into your usual shape?'

'Sure thing,' replied the shark, doing a thumbs up with one fin. Suddenly Sim was standing there in place of the shark.

Erika turned to face Chanda as they

walked out. 'See, I told you we'd find a way out!'

The ghost of a smile appeared on Chanda's lips. 'I suppose you did,' she said. 'Wait . . . what was that sound?'

Erika shrugged. 'What sound?'

'A kind of muffled, groaning sound. It sounds like . . . it's . . .' Chanda held her hand up and everyone fell silent. 'It's *underneath* us!'

'Oh no!' cried Erika. 'It'll be the guard!'

'Well, **come on**!' cried Chanda, leaping off the heavy door and trying to heave it up. 'We have to help him!'

'Er, he was keeping us prisoner, remember?' said Wade.

'But that doesn't mean we can just leave him like this,' exclaimed Chanda firmly. 'He could be hurt! Come on, help me move this door.'

The door was shoved to one side to reveal the crumpled shape of the guard. He sat up, grimacing and hissing in through his teeth as he cradled his left foot.

'Your foot?' said Chanda gently. The guard nodded. Chanda ripped off a long strip of fabric from her shirt and, with Beastling's help, began cleaning the cut and binding the guard's foot (although

Beastling's help mainly consisted of getting in the way a bit).

'Er . . . we kind of need to leave,' said Silas. 'Sort of *now*-ish.'

'Not until I've finished up here,' said Chanda, her jaw set defiantly. 'Go on without me if you have to.'

Silas looked at Wade, who looked at Erika.

'We'll wait,' said Erika, watching Chanda thoughtfully.

Before long, the foot was bound and the guard was looking gratefully at Chanda.

'Be sure not to put much weight on it,' she said. 'And get it looked at properly as soon as you can, OK?'

The guard nodded. 'Thank you,' he said quietly.

'So? Can we go now?' asked Silas.

'Absolutely!' replied Chanda.

'About time,' muttered Wade under his breath. 'Let's just hope we don't come across any more evil, dangerous creatures with minor injuries, otherwise we might **never** get out of here.'

'You know what though?' Erika said quietly to Wade. 'Seeing Chanda do that has just given me an idea of how we might finally solve this mission.'

CHAPTER 10

The **DREAM DEFENDERS** crept silently through the depths of the palace, pressed into dark corners like shadows. Sim had gone one step further and actually turned herself into a shadow – Wade's shadow. She was making it look like Wade's shadow was pulling funny faces at him behind his back, until Silas gave her a stern look and she started to behave herself.

While Beastling was telling his life story to Chanda in a series of incredibly detailed pictures, Erika whispered her plan to Wade, Silas and Sim.

'I don't know, Erika,' said Wade. 'It seems a bit risky to me.'

'I know it's risky!' replied Erika. 'But time's running out, remember? If we don't save Chanda in this Dreamcycle then the **DOUBT** is going to take over her life in my world, too. We have to do something!'

Wade and Silas looked at each other and then nodded in agreement.

'Looks like we have our plan then,' said Erika.

They found a quiet corner and Silas created a temporary invisibility shield around them all.

'So, we know that the **DOUBT** is in the throne room,' said Silas. 'There's some kind of protection that's blocking me from getting right inside, but I can teleport us close to it.' He glanced over at Chanda. 'We'll have a bit of a fight on our hands. But this time we'll be ready. You just stay with Erika and she'll make sure you're OK. Right, Erika?'

'Absolutely!' said Erika, grinning at Chanda. 'And we brought a few bits of gear from HQ to help out.' She held up what looked like a TV remote control. 'This is a Controller. It can pause, fast forward or rewind people. Look, I'll demonstrate.' She pointed the device at Silas and pressed the reverse button. There

was a dazzling electrical light
and Silas's eyes shot wide open.

**'It stop! Doing
you are what?'**
he gasped, moving
strangely until
Erika pressed the
play button.

'Just a quick
demonstration.'
She turned back to
face Chanda. 'Pretty
cool, right?' Chanda
nodded, her eyes
bright with excitement.

'And what about this?' she asked,
holding up a small green sphere, which
Sim had just passed to her.

'A whatever-you-want bomb,' said Sim. 'You throw it at your enemy and shout out a word while it's in the air. Wherever the bomb lands gets completely covered in whatever you called out. Look, I'll show you.' She tossed a bomb and called out, 'Nettles!'

There was a quiet *poof* followed by shouts and yelps.

'**AYYYYYYAAAGGGHHH!**' howled Wade from where the

bomb had just landed. 'Why would you do that!'

'Sorry!' called Sim, and she threw another whatever-you-want bomb shouting out, 'Dock leaves!'

'So, you see,' said Erika, 'we're not completely helpless. And we'll stick together, you and me.'

Chanda smiled. 'You and me,' she repeated. 'That sounds good.'

'We'll have to fight our way inside the throne room,' said Silas, 'getting past any enemies that we come across, and then weaken the **DOUBT** enough for Chanda to be able to take it on. Remember, she's the only one who can actually defeat it. Our job is to get her there safely, lay the groundwork and act as back-up. Everyone clear?'

'I don't know . . .' said Chanda, looking down and twisting her foot into the ground. 'What if I can't do it? What if I can't beat it?'

'Of course you can!' said Erika firmly. 'The **DOUBT** used to be a quiet little voice in your head – a tiny part of you. You are stronger than it and, deep down, you know that. It's scared of you – not the other way around. That's why it tries to keep you feeling so bad.'

'I . . . I don't think I'm ready,' whispered Chanda.

'We rarely feel ready for the challenges that are thrust upon us,' said Silas sagely. 'It's only by rising to those that are placed in our paths that we realize we are more capable than we may have initially thought.'

'Are you reading that from a book?' asked Erika suspiciously.

'What?' said Silas, hiding something behind his back. 'Of course not!'

'What's that then?' asked Erika.

'What?'

'That,' replied Erika, grabbing the book from behind Silas's back. She held it out and read the title. '*1001 Inspirational Things to Say to Make Yourself Seem Clever and Wise.*'

'Oh, that book,' said Silas sheepishly. 'Well, it does have some useful pointers.'

'Besides,' interrupted Wade, 'it's not like we have a choice! Chanda, if we don't defeat this creature before the end of the Dreamcycle then it's going to take over your entire life! So, you HAVE to—' He paused and looked at Erika, who was making '**STOP TALKING**' motions behind Chanda's back. Wade looked around awkwardly and then carried on talking in a new, soothing tone. 'Just be confident, calm and relaxed. You can totally do this, and we absolutely have your back.'

'Thanks, Wade!' said Chanda, patting the stone man on the arm. Erika let out a silent sigh of relief.

'Thanks for your help, all of you,' said Chanda, looking around at the group, her eyes shining. 'You're my best friends in the world!'

'Your best friends in *this* world,' said Silas, grinning. 'But there are loads of people back home who will want to be friends with you. You'll see! All we need to do is get rid of that **DOUBT'S** voice!'

'Absolutely,' agreed Erika. 'Let's go and get your dream back!'

Everybody whooped and cheered, apart from Wade who scowled and muttered, 'Oh, so you all cheer when Erika says it . . .'

CHAPTER 11

Erika blinked as Silas teleported them as close as he could to the **DOUBT**. Dizzying sensations swam nauseatingly around her. It always felt strange when Silas teleported them, but *usually* she had a few seconds to gather her thoughts. Not this time though.

A boxing glove flashed past Erika's head. She looked around and there, standing in front of her, blocking the corridor, was a huge kangaroo wearing shiny silk shorts and jabbing

its fists in the air.

'You don't stand a chance!' bragged the kangaroo, squaring up to Erika. 'I'll dismantle you! I'll give you a lesson in boxing you'll never forget! I'm in the best shape of my LIFE!' The kangaroo paused to flex its muscles. 'I've had twelve months of rigorous training. There is literally **NO WAY** you could beat me!'

Erika backed nervously away. 'OK, can we just talk about this?'

'The time for talking is **OVER!**' bellowed the kangaroo, jabbing a boxing glove in Erika's direction. It then rather undermined that statement by continuing to talk, at length, about what an amazing boxer it was.

Next to her, Silas rolled his eyes. 'They do this. *All. The. Time*,' he muttered. 'I don't think I've ever seen a boxing kangaroo actually do any boxing.'

'But how do we get past?' whispered Erika. 'He's massive!'

'I've got an idea . . .' muttered Wade. 'I was saving this for later, but what the heck!' He reached his stone hand inside the glowing round light in the middle of his chest and pulled out a large bag of jam doughnuts.

'Did you just PULL SOMETHING OUT OF YOUR OWN CHEST?' yelped Erika.

'Sure,' replied Wade. 'It's where I keep important things I think I might need on a mission.'

'So, what else have you got in there?' asked Erika excitedly.

'Er, nothing,' admitted Wade, looking flustered. 'Just the doughnuts. We left HQ in a hurry, remember?'

'Right . . .' said Erika.

Wade flushed slightly. 'Look, I really like doughnuts. And besides, I *knew* they'd come in handy.' He turned around and held out the doughnuts. The kangaroo's eyes followed the bag hungrily.

'Fancy a doughnut?' asked Wade.

'Er . . . no,' said the kangaroo. 'My trainer says I'm not allowed.'

'I don't see your trainer here,' said

Wade, popping a doughnut into his mouth. '*Mmmmmm*,' he murmured. 'That is *delicious*!'

The kangaroo didn't realize, but its tongue was lolling out.

'I *love* doughnuts!'

'Go on, treat yourself!' said Wade. 'One little doughnut's not going to hurt, is it?'

'I suppose not,' said the kangaroo, untying its boxing gloves.

'Take as many as you want,' said Wade enticingly. The kangaroo leaped forwards and scooped out a dozen doughnuts, putting three in his mouth at once. He leaned against the wall, eyes shut in pure, sugary bliss.

'That is **SO** good!' he mumbled with his mouth full. 'Thank you!'

'My pleasure!' said Wade, giving Erika an especially smug look as they crept past.

Silas led the way to the throne room, but the closer they got, the more enemies they faced. Books on the shelves leaped out, snapping their pages furiously as they hissed and spat, until Sim morphed into a strict librarian and gave them a *very* stern glare. They came up against a variety of **Hornheads, Cavesquarks, Venomtoes** and a slow-moving old lady

with massive shopping bags. She wasn't one of the enemies, she'd just got lost on her way back from another dream. The **DREAM DEFENDERS** took on all of these challenges, deftly overtaking the old lady with a chorus of '*excuse me*'s even though she was moving *incredibly* slowly and had A LOT of bags.

It wasn't long before they stood outside the throne room doors.

'Right!' said Erika. 'Is everybody ready?'

The **DREAM DEFENDERS** looked at each other and nodded. Even Chanda's eyes seemed bright and certain.

'Yes,' she replied.

Erika glanced over at Wade, who kicked the door open and burst in with Silas and Sim, ready to take on whatever enemies were inside.

But there was no one there – the throne room was empty. Wade looked around, scowling. As he did so, the room seemed to glitch and shudder, then everything inside began to flicker and vanish. Seconds later it was completely empty. Just a blank cell, with no windows, no doors and no furniture.

Silas turned to walk out, but was blocked by an invisible wall in the doorway. His eyes widened as he looked over at Wade and Sim.

'It's a trap!' gasped Wade. He spun round, striking the invisible wall with his fists. Nothing happened. Silas and Sim used their powers to help, but nothing that they tried worked. Erika took an old picture off the wall and poked it into the room. It went *in* easily enough, but when she tried to pull the painting back, the part of it that was in the cell fell on the floor and she was left holding half a painting.

'**WHOA!**' she

whispered. 'That's not good . . .'

'You'll have to go on without us,' said
Silas, a grim look on his face. 'I've no idea
how long it will take to get out of here.'

'OK,' said Erika, trying to sound
confident. She glanced over at Chanda
and smiled her brightest, most reassuring
smile. Given their current situation, it was
neither particularly bright nor especially
reassuring.

'Don't worry,' said Erika. 'I'm sure
we'll be fine. Now, come on, let's find the
real throne room!'

Wade slumped down in the featureless
room and watched as Erika, Beastling
and Chanda set off down the corridor.

'I hope you're right about this, Erika!'
he called out.

CHAPTER 12

There were multiple false doors leading into numerous horrible traps. One room led into a giant snake pit that was *doubly* horrible because the pit itself was made from snakes. But they weren't going to be caught out by the same trick twice. Erika, Chanda and Beastling took their time and eventually were able to work out which door led into the real throne room.

Beastling tapped Chanda on the arm and looked up at her, a concerned expression on his face as he created a picture of the letter 'Y' completely covered in red paint, and a question mark.

Chanda frowned as she inspected the image.

'He's asking if you're "Red-y".' explained Erika.

Chanda smiled at Beastling and ruffled the fur on his head. 'I'm as ready as I'll ever be,' she replied.

'OK,' said Erika. 'Here we go then.' She took a deep breath and opened the door.

There it was. The **DOUBT**. It reclined on the throne, one leg hung casually over the armrest.

'So, you finally got here?' it said. 'To be honest, I'm a little surprised. I thought you'd all get trapped.'

Chanda's face grew pale. She opened
her mouth to speak, but no words came
out. She took a step backwards, her fingers
trembling. Erika shot a glance over at

her friend and smiled reassuringly. Then she turned back to the **DOUBT** and her eyes narrowed.

'Listen to me!' said Erika. 'You're going to leave this castle, you're going to leave this dream and you're going to leave Chanda alone! She's not going to listen to you any more. Right, Chanda?'

Chanda's eyes were wide. Silently, she shook her head.

The **DOUBT** laughed so much that tears rolled down its cheeks. 'Oh, is that right?' it spluttered. 'And what makes you think that?'

'This!' replied Erika. She nodded at Beastling. Together they pulled out their Controllers, pointed them towards the **DOUBT** and pressed the pause button.

There was a crackling flash as two bright beams of energy lanced over towards the **DOUBT**, but nothing happened.

'Are you all complete idiots?' taunted the **DOUBT**. 'I'm not real – at least, not yet. You can't hurt me like that!'

Erika felt her temper rising. She gritted her teeth. 'Oh yeah? Well, how about this!' She grabbed three whatever-you-want bombs and threw them at the **DOUBT** yelling, 'Kindness!'

The bombs exploded and a hazy fog surrounded the **DOUBT**. It looked around frantically, eyes wide and desperate.

'Wha-what's happening?' it gasped.

Erika let out a relieved breath. The

whatever-you-want bombs had worked! 'You're feeling kindness,' she replied.

Unsteadily, the **DOUBT** rose out of the throne, glazed eyes swimming. 'Make it stop!' the creature called out pathetically. 'Help me, please.'

Erika glared at the **DOUBT**. 'First, you have to promise to leave Chanda alone.'

'OK, OK!' replied the **DOUBT**. 'Anything. Please, just make it stop.' It coughed and grimaced as it fell to its knees, thrashing about on the floor.

'Look, we don't want to hurt you,' said Erika, taking a step towards the stricken creature. 'We just want you to leave Chanda alone.'

'BIG MISTAKE!' yelled the **DOUBT**, reaching out to grab the remote control that was hanging at Erika's waist. It jabbed a finger down on the pause button. There was a jolt of energy and Erika and Beastling were frozen in place. Erika tried to struggle but it was no use – she was completely stuck. Her heart beat faster as the **DOUBT** spoke again.

'Seriously? That was your plan? You thought that you could defeat me with kindness? That's so pathetic it's almost funny! Now I can take over Chanda's waking life as well as her dreams, and there's no one who can stop me!'

'Yes, there is,' called out Chanda in a quiet voice. 'There's me.'

'Are you still here?' said the **DOUBT**, without even looking up.

'Boring, friendless Chanda. Can't you do everyone a favour and just get lost?'

'You're wrong,' said Chanda.

'What?' The **DOUBT** blinked as it looked up at Chanda. There was something different in her voice, she sounded stronger, more determined. 'I said you're *wrong*,' repeated Chanda firmly.

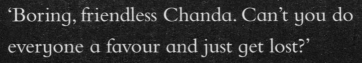

Go on, Chanda! thought Erika.

'You mean you're NOT boring and dull?' sneered the **DOUBT**. 'Come off it! I know what you're like, I used to be a part of you!'

'You're wrong that I don't have any friends,' said Chanda. 'These are my friends – and I won't let you hurt them. Any of them.'

'And how are you going to stop me?' sneered the **DOUBT**.

'I'm just going to ignore you,' said Chanda.

'What?' spluttered the **DOUBT**. 'That's ridiculous! Oh, just go and be feeble and miserable somewhere else!'

But Chanda didn't move.

'No,' she said.

'GO ON! GET OUT OF HERE!'
yelled the **DOUBT**, a ripple of fear running across its features.

'Look. Here's what's going to happen,' said Chanda coolly, her eyes fixed on the **DOUBT'S** face. '*You* are going to go away now. You're going to shrink away into nothing, because you don't have *any* power over me any more. I can see that now. You're nothing. You can say whatever you like, but you don't exist without me, so I'm *not* going to listen to you.'

'You don't have the strength!' said the **DOUBT**, attempting to sneer. 'You're weak, pathetic . . . you're . . .' But even as the creature spoke, it was fading away.

Soon there was just a pale, thin

impression of where the **DOUBT** *had* been. The sibilant hiss of its voice continued for a while, taunting Chanda, but even that was getting quieter and quieter, until soon there was nothing there at all.

CHAPTER 13

The throne room door crashed open and Wade, Silas and Sim burst in, just as Chanda was using the Controller to un-pause Erika and Beastling.

'It worked!' exclaimed Silas. 'The **DOUBT'S** gone. You did it, Erika!'

'No, Chanda did it,' replied Erika, grinning happily now that she could move again. 'Just like I knew she would! As soon as we were all captured and she was trying to rescue us rather than save herself, it changed everything!'

'You mean, you all got captured on purpose!' said Chanda, her eyes wide. 'But I thought you were in terrible danger!'

'We were,' insisted Erika. 'After all, we couldn't do anything to get rid of the **DOUBT** – it was only ever you that could stop it.'

'But . . . you tricked me,' said Chanda quietly.

'No,' replied Erika. 'We just helped you to see what you're capable of. Sometimes it's easier to be brave for someone else than it is to stand up for yourself.'

'And we were totally stuck in that prison!' added Sim. 'If you hadn't overcome the **DOUBT** we'd have been stuck there forever! You really did save us.'

Chanda smiled, and a curious expression

flickered over her face, as though she was considering herself in a new light.

'Yes,' she replied thoughtfully. 'I suppose I did.'

'To be honest, I didn't think it was going to work,' said Wade, with one eyebrow raised. 'But I've got to hand it to you Chanda – you did brilliantly. Well done!'

An alarm went off on Wade's watch and he looked around at the group.

'Is it that time already?' asked Sim.

'Looks like it!' replied Wade. 'Erika, we need to get you back to your dream, pronto, or you'll miss your chance to wake up.'

'Really, you all have to go now?' asked Chanda, looking crestfallen. 'But I'll miss you . . .'

'We'll miss you too!' said Erika, pulling her new friend into a tight hug. 'Just remember, you're *amazing*! You're kind, you're thoughtful and there's nothing you can't do if you set your mind to it! ***That's*** the voice you need to listen to. And if you ever hear those negative whispers again, just ignore them – OK? Just keep repeating the good things instead.'

'OK,' said Chanda, her eyes shining. 'Thanks, Erika.'

Beastling smiled as Chanda bent down and squeezed him up in her arms.

'We really need to go now,' said Wade, glancing at his watch.

'Just because you want to go back to HQ to get more doughnuts,' said Sim.

'No!' protested Wade, his cheeks flushing. 'I'm only thinking about getting Erika home safely.'

'Sure, Wade,' said Silas, grinning. 'Whatever you say . . . but we really had better go.' He patted Chanda on the back. 'Thanks again for saving us, and enjoy your dreams. This is all yours now – just as it's meant to be!'

Chanda ran over to the window and threw back the curtains. A huge double rainbow was floating in the sky above the town. She smiled as she looked out at

the wonderful
landscape and
the rollercoaster
that twisted its way
through the buildings.

'I think I'm going to have some real fun here!' she said, turning back to face her friends. 'Thank you all so much. Goodbye!'

Erika smiled happily and waved as Wade pressed a button on his wrist, and then the **DREAM DEFENDERS** faded away.

CHAPTER 14

zzzzzzzZzzzzT! zzzzzzzZZZZTT
TZZZZZZZZZZZZZZTTTTTTTT!
The alarm clock was buzzing in increasingly urgent tones. Erika smiled as she opened her eyes. It was all done — the mission had been a complete success. As soon as they were back at **DREAM DEFENDERS** HQ Silas had taken her back to the dream portals. The last thing she remembered was stepping back into her dream, and now, here she was . . .

Erika sprang out of bed and got ready

for school. After wolfing down breakfast she said goodbye to her parents and set off. It was the day of the talent show and she was excited to see who would win.

Erika clapped loudly as Darren Nicholson took a deep, soggy bow. His act hadn't gone especially well, but juggling with water was a *very* ambitious and unique idea. Mrs Lightfoot, the headmistress, squelched into the middle of the stage, wringing the water out of her cardigan (Darren's act really hadn't gone very well at all).

'Thank you, Darren,' she said in the tones of someone who wasn't really feeling all that thankful. 'And next up we have Kris Holmes, who's going to tell us some jokes. Take it away, Kris!'

Erika gasped. Kris had decided to enter the competition! She tried to do that really loud whistle where you stick two fingers in your mouth, but just made a soggy pffffftttttttttttttthhhhhhh sound. Erika frowned. That was clearly *another* skill she needed to master.

Kris walked awkwardly on to the stage. For a few seconds he just stood there. Silent. Looking nervously around.

'**Boooo!**' yelled an older boy's voice from the other end of the hall. 'This is rubbish!'

Erika's eyes shot wide open.

Mrs Lightfoot glared and was about to tell the heckler off when Kris tapped the microphone to make a loud **THUD** through the speakers.

'Sorry, am I in the right place?' he asked. 'I thought this was a school talent show, not the local zoo.' A ripple of laughter ran through the crowd.

'Well, go on,' said the boy, sounding embarrassed. 'Tell some jokes!'

'I think you're confused,' said Kris. 'My act is telling jokes, not talking to animals.' The audience laughed louder.

'You're not funny!' shouted the boy in the audience.

'Wait a minute! cried Kris. 'I have an animal–to–human translation guide here.' He took a piece of paper from his pocket and pretended to study it. 'I think what you just said was, "I'm going to be quiet now and let Kris carry on with his act".'

The audience burst into spontaneous applause and Kris began to visibly relax. 'So, I lost my dog at the beach the other day. There I was, shouting his name out at the top of my lungs and everyone ran away screaming! I guess I shouldn't have called my dog Shark . . .'

* ✸ ✸ ✸ ✸

When it was time to announce the winner, the crowd was already chanting '**KRIS! KRIS! KRIS!**' so it was no surprise to anyone when he won.

'Kris!' exclaimed Erika, running up to him after he received his trophy. 'That was amazing! You were so funny! And the way you dealt with that boy. I just . . . WOW! It was brilliant!'

'Thanks Erika!' said Kris, smiling broadly. 'But you know, I couldn't have done it without you.'

'Huh?' Erika's brows knitted together. 'What do you mean?'

'Oh, come off it,' laughed Kris. 'I *know* I was the mysterious "friend" you were talking about yesterday. It was obvious.

Well, anyway, I kept thinking about it and you were right – I can't feel scared about trying new things, you know? I've got to be a bit more confident!'

'Ah, right! Yeah, of course . . . *that* conversation . . .' said Erika, realizing how her conversation about Chanda would have sounded to Kris. 'Yeah, that's, er, totally what I meant!' Her cheeks and ears turned pink.

'Well, it worked!' said Kris happily. 'So, thanks a lot!'

'It really was all you!' protested Erika. 'Still, I'm so glad you entered *and* won! You were brilliant!'

The two friends grinned at each other as they bustled down the crowded corridors to find their bags and walk home.

That evening, as Erika was getting ready for bed, she felt a tingle from the **DREAM CRYSTAL** around her neck. She ran to the mirror and took out the necklace, which was glowing brightly — a message from the Dreamscape!

'Erika,' rang out Madam Hettyforth's voice. 'I just wanted to say, well done! What a brilliant idea! It takes real strength and leadership to let someone else be the hero, and in Chanda's case, it was just what she needed. I thought you might like to see this clip of Chanda from the Lacunascope. Wait a second . . . Silas? How the *woolly-word* do you work this thing again?' There was silence for a few seconds and then Ma'am's voice started again. 'Aha! Like that is it? Can't they make these things simpler? Anyway, I'm beaming it over now. Once again well done, Erika!'

A bright light shot out of the crystal and filled the surface of the mirror as though it was a TV screen. It showed Chanda in her waking life, and there was Inu, the girl who had been so unkind before. She marched up to Chanda in the queue for lunch and pushed in front of her.

'You don't mind if I go in front do you?' said Inu, without waiting for a response. 'Did you do anything fun last night?' She let out a tinkling laugh, as though she and Chanda really were friends and were actually having a nice time.

'Actually, Inu, I did,' replied Chanda.

'I learned an important lesson.'

'Oh yes?' replied Inu, sounding bored. 'And what was that? How to tie your shoelaces?'

'No,' replied Chanda calmly. 'I learned that I don't need to listen to mean, hurtful voices. I learned what it means to have real friends, and I learned that you're no happier than me – otherwise you wouldn't treat me the way you do. So, if you ever want to try to be a better person I'm happy to help, but for now, please go and take your place at the back of the queue.'

Everyone turned to watch, mouths hanging open. Inu stood there blinking.

'**Now,** please, Inu,' added Chanda. 'You're holding everybody up.'

Unable to think of anything to say, Inu slowly turned and walked to the back of the queue.

'How did you do that, Chanda?' asked a thin boy with large brown eyes. 'I don't think anyone's ever stood up to Inu before!'

'Something happened last night,' replied Chanda, frowning. 'In my dreams . . . I can't remember exactly what it was, but when I woke up this morning I decided that nobody was ever going to push me around again.'

'Can you help me to feel like that?' asked the boy cautiously.

'Of course,' replied Chanda, smiling. 'What are friends for?'

Erika whooped and clapped as the clip ended and the glow from the necklace faded away – everything had worked out perfectly.

'What's going on?' demanded her mum, poking her head round the door. 'Randall's only just got to sleep!'

'Oh, sorry, Mum,' said Erika. 'I was just practising my, er . . . seal impression.' She clapped her hands together like flippers and waddled around the room making a low honking sound.

'You know what? That's actually very good,' said her mum. 'You really do look *and* sound like a seal.'

'Really?' asked Erika.

'Yeah!' Her mum laughed. 'It's funny, too. If you keep practising you could enter the next talent show yourself! Now, come on! Time for bed. It'll be another busy day tomorrow and you need a calm, restful night's sleep.'

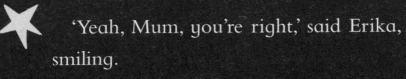

'Yeah, Mum, you're right,' said Erika, smiling.

Her time spent sleeping was a lot of things, but "calm" and "restful" were probably *not* the words that she would choose.

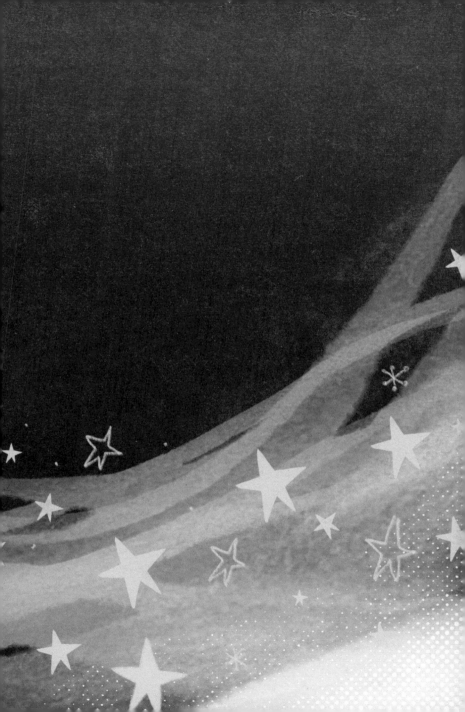

Turn the page to read a sneak peek
from the third **DREAM DEFENDERS**
adventure *Silas and the Marvellous Misfits* –
a **Marcus Rashford Book Club Choice**!

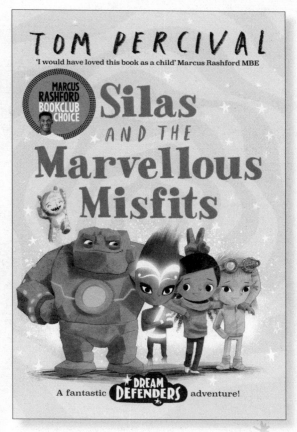

CHAPTER 1

Erika swam upwards through a cloud
that smelled strongly of marshmallows.
She glanced over at Beastling,
swimming along beside her.
He smiled and mumbled,
'**Heebie Jeebie**,' through
the thickening cloud.

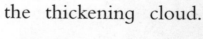

As he spoke, a speech bubble popped out of his mouth, showing a picture of a thumbs up and a smiley face. Erika grinned and looked down at her timer. Twenty-five seconds. That was all they had before the cloud turned into a marshmallow and plunged to the ground in a deadly (but completely delicious) mess. This was not something that Erika wanted to happen – at least, not with them still inside the cloud!

BZZZZZT!

Erika's communications device buzzed and a gravelly voice spoke. 'Hey, Erika.

2

Listen, while you're back at Head Quarters getting that truth cannon, can you bring me a couple of doughnuts please?'

'What?' gasped Erika, struggling not to breathe in too much marshmallow. 'Look, Wade, I'm kind of busy right now!'

'Oh yeah, of course,' replied Wade. 'Sorry. And good luck!' There was a pause. 'But don't forget the doughnuts.' Then he ended the call.

Erika shook her head and swam faster.

Seventeen seconds later, Erika and Beastling popped out the top of the cloud, just as it became too thick to swim through. They sprinted to the edge and leaped off as the marshmallow cloud began to tumble towards the ground far below. Beastling followed close behind her. He *had* to. Erika and Beastling were bonded together, which meant that they could only ever be a few metres apart from each other. It had been that way since Erika's first adventure in the Dreamscape. Well, technically, it was ever since Beastling had first *bitten* her that they'd been bonded together – but that was a long time ago, and there was no point getting upset about it now.

Cold wind tore at Erika's skin as Beastling manoeuvred himself through the air and grabbed her shoulders. She thrust her arms and legs out in a star

shape and glowing sheets of
light spread between her hands
and feet like wings, creating a flying
suit that Erika could steer and control.

'Only the best for the **DREAM
DEFENDERS**, right?' yelled Erika, grinning.
If she tried to tell her friends at school

about any of this they would think she had gone mad! It wasn't like you could just say, 'By the way, I'm part of the **DREAM DEFENDERS**, a top-secret organization that helps children solve any problems they're having in their dreams.'

Her friends hadn't even believed her when she said her uncle had a Ferrari, so there was NO WAY they'd believe any of *this*!

To be fair to Erika's friends, her uncle *didn't* have a Ferrari. But he did have a red car that looked kind of sporty.

Erika twisted her body around, steering them towards the flattened top of an upside-down mountain in the distance. She looked at the impossible world around her as they shot through the air: far below a forest grew on the underside of a nearby cloud. The Dreamscape really was an amazing place.

A couple of seconds later they landed on the top of the mountain.

'**Heebie Jeebie!**' cried Beastling, punching the air excitedly. A speech bubble appeared with a picture of a female sheep and a cheese grater in it. Erika smiled and ruffled Beastling's fur.

'Ewe grate too!' she said with a grin. 'Let's get inside and find the others!'

Erika and Beastling crept down a roughly carved set of steps leading deep within the mountain. Damp, stale air drifted lazily down the corridor as Erika peered around.

'Where is everyone?' she muttered. 'This is where we were supposed to meet.'

'*Psst* . . . Erika!' a voice suddenly whispered from behind her.

Erika yelped and spun around – there was nobody there.

'Sorry!' continued the voice hastily. 'I didn't mean to startle you. I know it can be dangerous for a human's heartbeat to become too elevated. Do you want me to hum some soothing music?' The disembodied voice stopped speaking and started humming. Badly.

'Silas?' interrupted Erika. 'Is that you? Why are you invisible? And *please* stop humming.'

The humming stopped. 'Oh. Am I still invisible?'

'*Yes!*' replied Erika.

'Ah! Right. Give me a second . . .' The air shimmered and suddenly the drifting, insubstantial figure of a boy appeared. Swirls of light covered his face and body, and even when he was fully visible he still faded away to nothing just below the knees.

'Ta-daaaa!'
exclaimed Silas.
'Better?'
'Much better!' said Erika.
'So, have you worked out how
to solve Miles's problem
yet?'

Silas shook his head. 'Not yet, but *hopefully* the truth cannon will help! Did you get it?'

Erika nodded and Beastling pointed to the weighty backpacks they were both carrying.

'Great!' exclaimed Silas. 'Wade and Sim have gone ahead to the centre of the mountain with Miles. That's where all the negative energy is coming from.'

'So, what are we waiting for?' asked Erika. 'Let's go!'

To be continued . . .

Meet the ★ DREAM DEFENDERS

They're on a mission to banish your worries while you sleep!

TOM PERCIVAL

They're on a mission to banish the worries!

Chanda
AND THE
Devious
Doubt

A fantastic DREAM DEFENDERS

TOM PERCIVAL

'I would have loved this book as a child' Marcus Rashford MBE

Silas
AND THE
Marvellous
Misfits

A fantastic DREAM DEFENDERS adventure!

ACKNOWLEDGEMENTS

One thing that I get asked a lot at school visits and festival events is, 'Where do you get your ideas from?' I'm not alone in this, I'm pretty sure that all authors get asked it. The trouble is that most authors don't *want* to tell people where they got their ideas from. This is fair enough though, because come on, let's face it . . . If YOU were lucky enough to find a magic 'ideas' tree growing in a secluded glade in a forest in mid-Wales then you'd probably want to keep it a secret too! So there you go . . . All authors have a magic ideas tree. Now you just need to ask them WHERE their secret ideas tree is hidden . . .

However, magic trees aside, in the case of this book I can tell you *exactly* where some of the ideas came from - my kids. My youngest child

Joey drew sketches of various monsters and wrote detailed descriptions of them, too. And so were born, Dragon Whales, Hornheads and of course the dreaded Bone Cobble! My eldest, Ash, is drawn to the more cutesy end of the imagination spectrum and influenced the gentler parts of Chanda's dream world and her general, undeniable 'goodness'. So 'thanks' kids, but don't expect any payment! Me and your mum pay for the all the food, the bills, the mortgage and we bought the games console and ALL YOUR BOOKS so I think it's only fair that you give your poor old dad a few ideas from time to time.

A final 'ideas' credit goes to Ewan. On a camping trip that my family took with some of our friends, their son Ewan told me that I HAD to include a boxing kangaroo in this book. He was VERY insistent and reminded me about it whenever he saw me picking up my kids from school and in the end I realized that I was going to have to write in a boxing kangaroo, or there would be trouble. So there you go, persistence pays off.

And finally MERRY CHRISTMAS! I'm *so* happy that you received everything that you wanted.★

T.P.
May 2020

★ This assumes that you are reading this book on Christmas Day after having put it at the VERY top of your Christmas wish list. If this *isn't* the case then this final part of the message does not apply to you, please feel free to ignore it. Thanks and best wishes, Tom Percival.

ABOUT THE AUTHOR

Tom Percival writes and illustrates all sorts of children's books. He has produced cover illustrations for the 'Skulduggery Pleasant' series, written and illustrated the 'Little Legends' series, the 'Dream Defenders' series, as well as twelve picture books. His 'Big Bright Feelings' picture book series includes the Kate Greenaway-nominated *Ruby's Worry*, as well as *Perfectly Norman* and *Ravi's Roar*. *The Invisible* is a powerful picture book exploring poverty and those who are overlooked in our society. In 2020 he created the animation Goodbye Rainclouds, for BBC Children in Need to celebrate unsung heroes and launch their campaign. He lives in Gloucestershire with his partner and their two children.